This book belongs to:

_____

UNITED TALES OF AMERICA

EVERY STATE HAS A STORY

Written by Suzy Duffy - Illustrated by Mike Roberts

The Maine Migglenut is from a collection called **United Tales of America.**

There once was a bee
who sheltered from rain,
in a pine tree,
in a forest in Maine.

"Well, how do you do?" somebody said,
making the honeybee twizzle her head.

"I am a Migglenut. This is my home."
Then Honeybee asked, "And are you a cone?"

The Migglenut giggled.
"Who really can tell?
I'm cone and I'm nut,
but I'm berry as well!
A name doesn't matter,
I'm sure you agree,
when it's laughter
we're after
in life, Honeybee."

But Bee didn't share the nut's point of view.
"We Honeybees have much work to do.
I don't have time for you and your funny.
My life's important,
as I'm making honey."

She picked up her pot. "So, I must get going. The pollen is high and flowers are growing."

"Stop!" said the nut. "If you leave this tree.
It's likely you'll never again talk to me."

"I'm sure," said the bee,
"I could redo my flight."

"Perhaps," said the nut.
"You could be right.
But *I* may be gone to some other tree.
Today is our day, to chat, Honeybee."

Bee then accepted the nut's invitation,
And sat to discuss discombobulation.

While honey production was *her* number one,
she was intrigued by the concept of fun.

Migglenut talked
about laughing at life,
how giggles and chuckles
eliminate strife.

Bee started to question
the way of the hive.
"We work till we drop—
every day we're alive."

The Migglenut giggled. "I'll show you a way,
to brighten your life, just do as I say.
Take a deep breath, down into your tummy.
Then mix with a thought that you think is funny.

When you start to feel
a grin on your face,
the magic of mirth
is now taking place.

The giggles
are growing.

There's simply
no doubt.
All you need do,
is let 'em all out."

So, Bee took a breath
and closing her eyes,
tried to think funny
and to her surprise...

While dreaming of honey
and flying about,
it bubbled right up.

A giggle popped out!

"I'm feeling the mirth."
Bee's grin opened wide.
"I've chuckles, and chortles.
I'm mirthy inside!

You've made me so happy today,"
said the bee.
"I think you've invented
laughter therapy."

The Migglenut giggled.
"Then my work is done.
Just always remember
to make your own fun.

And when you feel down, if life is that bad,
Well, make something up and pretend to be glad.

Strange though it seems,
but after a laugh,

Problems and worries?
They all seem to half."

A long time has passed
since that auspicious date,
And today Maine is known as
'The Pine Tree State.'

And as for The Migglenut?
He's doing good.
Still sharing mirth with his friends
in his wood.

And Honeybee, too.
She gave such respect—
she's now the official
State Insect.

So let's all remember -
when life's in a rut
to make our own mirth,
like The Maine Migglenut.

The End

What do you think?

- Why do you think Bee was in a hurry at the start of the story?

- Can you remember what Migglenut suggested we do, if we have nothing to laugh about?

- Do you have ways to make yourself laugh?

- How would you make a friend laugh?

Fun Facts

- Maine is the first state in the USA to see sunlight every day because it's in the tip-top right-hand corner of the United States.

- There are over 4,000 islands off the coast of Maine!

- The largest city in Maine is Portland, and the State Capital is Augusta.

- It borders New Hampshire to the west and the Canadian provinces of New Brunswick and Quebec to the northeast and northwest.

Can you draw Migglenut?

Can you draw Bee?

Can you find
Maine state?

What other
states do you
know?

Color the states
you recognize.

Educator's page

Dear Educator,

At United Tales, we're dedicated to educating and empowering children as we entertain them.

- If you want more United Tales fairy tales for your classroom, please head to UnitedTalesOfAmerica.com. Your students can click on our interactive map of the USA to choose the story they want to watch and maybe, they'll learn a little geography too!

- To book a classroom Zoom visit, contact us through website.

United Tales of America

At United Tales, each story is set in a unique American state. It presents a specific life skill with an original, adorable character. Click on the State & Story you want to visit on our interactive map!

Collector's page

Are you collecting all the fairy tales for all the States in the USA?

To help you, here are the books we've published so far and a blank box for you to tick them off, as you acquire them.

Happy collecting!

Want more fairy tales?
Head to our website using this QR code. ⟶

www.ingramcontent.com/pod-product-compliance
Lightning Source LLC
Chambersburg PA
CBHW041004170626
46815CB00002B/154